Stewart Stork

by Ross Martin Madsen
pictures by Megan Halsey

DIAL BOOKS FOR YOUNG READERS · NEW YORK

Published by
Dial Books for Young Readers
A Division of Penguin Books USA Inc.
375 Hudson Street
New York, New York 10014

Text copyright © 1993 by Ross Martin Madsen
Pictures copyright © 1993 by Megan Halsey
All rights reserved
Design by Judy Lanfredi
Printed in Hong Kong by
South China Printing Company (1988) Limited

Library of Congress Cataloging in Publication Data
Madsen, Ross Martin.
Stewart Stork / by Ross Martin Madsen
pictures by Megan Halsey.
—1st ed.
p.   cm.
Summary: When Stewart Stork tries to become taller, faster, and stronger,
his friends help him realize that he is fine
just the way he is.
ISBN 0-8037-1325-8.—ISBN 0-8037-1326-6 (lib. bdg.)
[1. Self-acceptance—Fiction. 2. Storks—Fiction. 3. Animals—Fiction.]
I. Halsey, Megan, ill. II. Title.
PZ7.M2664St   1993   [E]—dc20   92-30730   CIP   AC

First Edition
1 3 5 7 9 10 8 6 4 2

The art for each picture consists of an ink, colored pencil,
dye, and watercolor painting.

Reading Level: 2.4

E
MADS

To Eleanor,
my Wild Irish Rose

R.M.M.

For my brother,
Super Jeff

M.H.

CONTENTS

TALLER, FASTER, AND STRONGER

Stewart closed his comic book,

and looked at himself in the mirror.

He felt sad.

He was not tall or fast or strong

like Superstork.

Even his friends were taller,

faster, and stronger.

"I am tall," said Stewart,

standing on his two long legs,

"but I can't see over the fence

at the ballpark like Gerald Giraffe.

"I have to climb up his neck

and sit on his head to watch the game.

"I can fly," Stewart said,

moving his wings,

"but not as fast as Howard Hummingbird.

He flies rings around me.

When I try to keep up,

my wings and legs get tangled.

"I am strong," said Stewart,

feeling his muscle,

"but not like Ellen Elephant.

She can hold me over her head

with her trunk, and I can't get free.

When I try to pick her up,

all I get are bent feathers.

" There are so many things

wrong with me.

"I want to be taller, faster,

and stronger just like Superstork."

STORK ON STILTS

Next day Stewart got an idea.

STILTS! He would make

the longest stilts in the world

and be taller than Gerald Giraffe;

taller than Superstork;

taller than anyone!

Stewart got some boards

and nailed them together.

"I am still not tall enough," he said

when he tried the stilts.

So he nailed on more and more boards

until he had the longest stilts

that had ever been made.

But they were so long

he could not get them on.

"Lean the stilts against me,"

said Gerald, "and climb up my neck.

You can sit on my head

and tie them onto your legs."

Stewart did,

and when he stood he was *very* tall.

Gerald cheered,

Howard hummed,

and Ellen blew long, loud hoots

through her trunk.

Stewart tried to take a step.

He could not move the stilts.

They were much too heavy,

and he started to fall.

"Ahhhhh!" he screamed as he headed

beak-first toward the ground.

Ellen caught him with her trunk
just before he hit.

"I think I am tall enough,"
Stewart said
when he finally opened one eye.

STORK ON WHEELS

"Superstork would win this race,
and so will I," said Stewart
as he tried on his new Rollerblades.
"These will make me faster," he said.

"Where are *your* Rollerblades?"

Stewart asked Howard Hummingbird.

"Skates would only slow me down,"

said Howard.

"I will wait at the starting line.

You can have a rolling start,"

and Howard zipped down the hill

toward the beach.

"Have you ever used Rollerblades?"
asked Gerald.

"No, but I am sure they will make me
faster than Howard," said Stewart.

"By the time I get to the start,
I will be going so fast
Howard will never catch me—
no matter how hard he flies.
Give me a push. Here I go!"

Stewart started down the hill.

He was soon out of control.

When he flashed by the starting line,
Ellen shouted, "Go!"

The race began.

Stewart shot down the sidewalk
and headed for the boat dock.

Howard flew behind him.

"Look out!" Howard shouted.

Stewart was lucky he had long legs

when a baby stroller got in his way.

He was unlucky when the banner

telling about the yearly beach party

wrapped around his face,

and when he ran out of sidewalk

at the end of the boat dock.

Stewart was lucky when he landed

in a pile of fish on a passing boat.

Stewart thanked the owner

for saving his life.

"Nice race," said Howard.

"Maybe I am fast enough

without Rollerblades," said Stewart.

MUSCLES FOR STORK

"I will lift weights," said Stewart.

"That will make me strong

like Superstork."

He got Gerald to drop two ropes

over the branch of a tree.

He had Ellen move a large rock

under the tree branch.

She held the rock in the air

while he tied the two ropes around it.

Stewart put the other ends
of the ropes around his wings
and began to pull.

The rock would not move.
"Let go and I will keep it up
in the air," said Stewart.

30

Ellen dropped the rock.

It fell to the ground

and Stewart shot into the air.

He crashed into the bottom

of a low-flying airplane,

tumbled through a flock of birds,

and landed in a haystack

a block and a half away

from the tree.

When Gerald, Ellen, and Howard
caught up to Stewart, Howard said,
"You really flew faster
than I could that time."
Stewart did not say anything.

He was too busy pulling the hay
out of his beak.

SATISFIED STORK

Stewart Stork learned

he was too small

to use tall stilts.

They were not safe,

so he made firewood out of them.

Stewart could tell

he was too slow

to beat Howard Hummingbird

in a race,

so he gave his new Rollerblades

to the boat owner's little girl.

Stewart found out

he was not strong enough

to lift large stones,

so he made a sign,

and put it next to the big rock.

It said For Climbing Only!

Stewart had not changed.

"I still *want* to be

taller, faster, and stronger,"

Stewart said.

"You *are* taller and stronger than me,"

said Howard.

"You *are* faster than me,"

said Ellen.

"And besides," said Gerald,

"you are the funniest stork

I have ever seen."

"We like you just the way you are,"

his friends said together.

Being taller, faster, and stronger

did not seem as important anymore.

"You know, Gerald," said Stewart,

"you are right. I am funny."